CAN A COOKIE
CHANGE THE WORLD?

Written and Interior Layout & Design by Rhon

Interior Illustrations by Gabrijela Sklep

Cover Illustrations & Design by Tamara Kokic • www.

This book is dedicated to:

Sandy Wendte

Who is courageously and graciously fighting ALS and inspiring those around her in more ways than she can ever imagine. The strength and legacy she has shared with the world are priceless gifts.

Thank You!

A special thank you to some of my wonderful and brilliant friends and family who helped contribute to this book by reading, encouraging, editing, and giving helpful suggestions. Words cannot convey the depth of my appreciation. God bless each of you.

Bill Bolling, Emily Bolling, Katie Bolling, David Branderhorst (BAE), Rebecca Brown, Heather Carr, M.T. Cobblepott (aka Suzan Thompson), Julie Douglas, Jenny Gore Dwyer, Christina Hubbard, Taylor Knight, Jessica Mathews, Lynn McWhorter, Jill Miller, Michelle Nezat, Kary Oberbrunner (AAE), Darla Riggan, Angela Salazar, Tessa Salazar, Katy Suiter, Susan Zartman, and the AWESOME members of the Igniting Souls Tribe.

© 2018 by Rhonda Bolling and Author Academy Elite:
Paperback: 978-1-64085-232-7
Hardback: 978-1-64085-233-4
Ebook: 978-1-64085-234-1

Library of Congress Control Number: 2018934197

All rights reserved.
Printed in the United States of America
Published by Author Academy Elite
P.O. Box 43, Powell, OH 43035

FOREWORD BY JENNY GORE DWYER

As a widow of an amazing man I lost to ALS in 2013, I am so honored to write the foreword for *Can a Cookie Change the World?* More than that, I'm so proud of the work Tessa has done to raise funds for special causes and ecstatic about this book's potential.

Rhonda Bolling's book about Tessa will inspire kids that they do have a voice and can make a difference. In addition, 70% of the proceeds will be donated, with 35% going to ALS Therapy Development Institute (*ALS TDI*), and 35% to *Kids' Cookies for a Cause* (for whatever Tessa chooses to donate to each year). The good that can come is unending.

In 2013, the year my handsome husband Patrick Dwyer passed away from ALS, I was nominated and confirmed to serve on the board of Directors for *ALS TDI*, which is the world's largest ALS-only research lab. All monies donated from this book or otherwise will be used solely for ALS research.

I am so happy to see that this book is dedicated to Tessa's Grandma Sandy, who was diagnosed with ALS in 2012. I am thrilled and honored that Tessa chose *ALS TDI* as one of her causes to support. Tessa's cause through Rhonda's book, will continue to fund ALS research, in honor of Tessa's grandmother, Sandy.

My husband Pat was an incredible, father, son, brother, uncle and friend. He lived life with ALS for 8 years with steadfast courage and humor. We miss him every day. Pat fully believed that a treatment for ALS would be found by the brilliant scientists at *ALS TDI*. He, and I, are so happy to know that through his connection to this horrible disease, good will come. Every dollar donated through *Can a Cookie Change the World?* will help find a treatment for ALS.

Those cookies made in Alaska, those heartfelt dollars raised for *ALS TDI*, the love baked into those dreams will one day reach the whole world, when an ALS treatment is found. Tessa and Rhonda, my thanks to you both is profound and immeasurable.

Tessa's story of how one girl with a big dream wanting to make a difference in her small Alaska hometown will make you smile, cry, and love. Rhonda's gracious storytelling sets the scene for children to be inspired, to care, and be aware that they can make a difference in this world...even through a cookie.

I highly recommend this book and encourage you to purchase it. Once you have it, grab a cookie and read away. Your tummy and your soul will be filled.

Jenny Gore Dwyer

www.fvbrennaa.com http://crabbymama.weebly.com/blog
https://www.als.net/about-als-tdi/als-tdi-board-of-directors/   www.als.net

More cool info: Jenny's son is Sean Dwyer who is the newest and youngest captain on the Deadliest Catch at https://www.als.net/captainsean/

Tessa's chocolate chip cookies filled her whole house with the scent of their just-baked goodness. On her list of favorite things to do, baking was close to the top. Lately, she had been thinking of ways to help some people in her community. She took a warm plate of cookies up to her room. Maybe she was too young to really make a difference, but she kept thinking.

She got dressed for the day and went downstairs. She had an idea that she wanted to run by her parents.

"Mom, Dad," Tessa said, "I'd like to do something to help the homeless people in our town. What if I had a table at the mall for the Christmas Bazaar and asked for donations that we could give to the homeless shelter?"

"That sounds like a great idea. Would you give anything in return for donations?" Tessa's mom asked.

"I could give them a cookie . . ." Tessa suggested as she thought the idea through, ". . . or maybe a bag of cookies if they donate a larger amount."

RECIPE CARD

Slice of spice cookies
1¼ c butter   1 cup sugar
1 c brown sugar   3¾ c flour
2 tsp cinnamon   1 tsp salt
1 tsp baking soda 1 tsp clove
1 tsp ground all spice

Since she had been very young, Tessa's determination and strong work ethic were evident to her parents. When she set her mind to something, she followed it through. Her parents were happy to encourage and support
this idea she had.

Since the Christmas Bazaar was only a few weeks away, they had a lot of work to do. She set a goal to make 600 cookies. They pulled out their favorite family recipes and checked their inventory of supplies. They would need huge bags of flour and sugar, and lots of eggs and butter.
With their list in-hand, they drove to the
grocery store to get started.

After a weekend of baking with her mom, Tessa called some friends to tell them about her idea. Since they had time off from school for Christmas break, they asked if Tessa wanted help, and of course, she was so happy to have their company and extra hands. They got together at Tessa's house and spent hours frosting cookies. Stiff backs and tired arms may have slowed them down a bit, but it didn't stop them. After decorating all the cookies, Tessa decided it would be fun to add different cookie recipes and all kinds of other treats, like cupcakes, cake pops, chocolate-dipped pretzels, and more! It was easy to get excited and keep thinking of new things they could have at their table.

Grandpa Ron pitched in, too! Usually, Grandma Sandy was the queen caramel-corn maker, but since her ALS* had progressed, she was only able to wear the supervisor hat as Tessa and Grandpa Ron whipped up the secret recipe. Bags and bags of caramel corn lined all the counters in Tessa's grandparent's kitchen. Tessa was sure this would be a hot commodity at her table as it had been a family favorite for as long as she could remember.

"Grandpa and Grandma," Tessa asked,
"Do you like the name 'Kids' Cookies for a Cause'
for my fundraising project?"
Her grandparents agreed it was the perfect name.

Only four days remained until the Christmas Bazaar.

*A quick note on ALS: ALS is short for Amyotrophic Lateral Sclerosis and also called Lou Gehrig's disease. It is a neurodegenerative disease that causes rapidly progressive muscle weakness. Specifically, the disease affects nerve cells (motor neurons) that control the muscles that enable you to move, speak, breathe and swallow. ALS-tdi is the Therapy Development Institute dedicated to finding a cure for ALS. https://www.als.net/

Please see the Glossary in the back of the book for all the causes mentioned and some of the difficult words.

Finally, the date circled in red marker on the calendar arrived, and wow, was Tessa ever nervous! What if no one showed up? What if she didn't make any money for the homeless shelter? She had all the normal, scary thoughts most people do when they try new things. Could she really make a difference? Would all the hard work be worth it? She decided to replace the negative thoughts with positive ones. She prepared for this and it was going to be a great day! She just knew it.

With their car jam-packed, they arrived at the mall early to set up. They unloaded bin after bin of cookies and supplies. Posters were hung and the treat table was ready. Then their first customer showed up...and they just kept coming. "What a great idea," some said. Others said, "Where's the famous caramel corn?" As the donations flowed in, the cookies and treats flowed out. Within four hours, their table was empty and the cash box was overflowing.
This is what Tessa had prayed for.

Over $1,000 was made for the homeless shelter that day. Tessa's dad matched her fundraising that year so she had twice the amount to give to the Homeless Shelter, which enabled them to purchase food, bedding supplies and warm winter clothes and gloves to give away when needed. They even bought a few small appliances for the shelter.

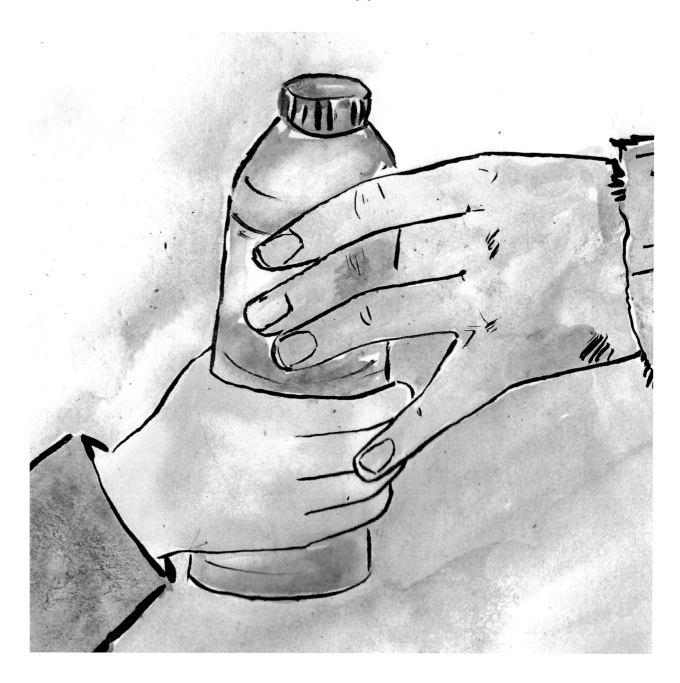

Not too many weeks later, she noticed a homeless man she had seen several times before. He wasn't wearing the old, worn out clothes and boots she had seen him wearing in the past, but much newer and warmer winter gear. She even thought she saw him smiling. Happy tears formed in Tessa's eyes. Their work had undoubtedly helped quite a few people. She definitely wanted to do it again. Could she make even more of a difference now that she knew what to do?

A few months after Tessa's first fundraiser, her friend Shelby got very sick. She was having a hard time at school and often felt tired and sick to her stomach. She was losing weight and drank water like a camel. Then, the doctors figured out that she had diabetes. Shelby cried. Her family cried, too. She would need to poke her finger many times a day to test her blood sugar and learn how to give herself insulin injections. They would work towards an insulin pump that would be attached to Shelby's body so she would not have to have so many shots. Tessa decided she would do another fundraiser at the next Christmas Bazaar and this time it would benefit Diabetes Education so she could help more kids like Shelby.

With experience as her helper, Tessa wrote a list of what she'd need to prepare for the next Christmas Bazaar. She started several months ahead of time and froze dozens of cookies, cakes, and candies. Her mom helped her order festive packaging in bulk quantities and even set up a Facebook page for "Kids' Cookies for a Cause." More friends joined in the efforts. She still didn't know how much her fundraising project would help, but she definitely didn't want to give up. She kept a positive attitude and worked hard.

The second year that Tessa had her treat table at the mall, she raised even more than the first year. It was so encouraging to give people a way to help others. Not only were they helping Tessa with her project, but they were affecting many, many people involved with the cause they were supporting. She wanted to continue to fund more projects and kept a constant eye out for those who needed help.

Well, you remember Grandma Sandy, right? Tessa's Grandma was very special to her. What her grandma was going through with ALS made those who knew her very sad. Grandma Sandy had always been the one to plan big family dinners and was warm and welcoming to all. People respected her for her kindness, wisdom, and positive attitude. Grandma Sandy had taught Tessa's mom how to be strong, and Tessa's mom taught Tessa to be strong. Tessa learned early in life that a positive attitude was crucial to success and happiness.

She also knew she wanted to raise money for "ALS Therapy Development Institute (TDI)," to help find a cure for ALS in honor of her Grandma.

Throughout the year, Tessa planned carefully. She raised money with yard sales and took donations for supplies. She had her recipes organized by when she would bake them and mapped everything, including her marketing plan, on a big calendar.

Rental of the school's kitchen for a few nights made it possible for a mass cookie production!

Grandma Sandy had so many friends who cooked for Tessa's table that year. More cookies, cakes, chocolate-dipped pretzels, candies, and caramel corn were donated than ever before! Because Tessa kept showing up year after year, her table was popular and people were excited to support the mission of "Kids' Cookies for a Cause." People flowed in by the hundreds to support ALS at Tessa's treat table. You'd never guess that they could raise over $9000, but that's exactly what happened!

She couldn't wait to tell Grandma Sandy the amazing news!

LET ME WIN. BUT IF I CANNOT WIN, LET ME BE BRAVE IN THE ATTEMPT. SPECIAL OLYMPICS OATH

Tessa continued supporting great causes by giving to Special Olympics the next year. She had several friends whose yearly highlight was to participate in the Special Olympics Games. Training all year with swimming, running, biking and all kinds of exercises prepared the athletes for competition and encouraged them to dream as they aimed for their goals. Their struggles built strength and determination. The losses taught them always to keep trying, and the victories

were triumphant and joyful. All of it brought celebration, fun, and memorable experiences with family and friends. The expensive travel, however, was a huge burden to many participants and Tessa knew her help would go to great use. She was incredibly honored to give to Special Olympics.

There was never a shortage of those needing help. Tessa wanted to help them all but chose for her fifth year to fundraise for a sweet, six-year-old girl named Lexi.

For a long time, Lexi's parents and her doctors couldn't figure out why she was so sick and in such horrible pain. Then, they discovered she had a rare disease called CRMO. That disease caused her bones to easily break and for her body to always hurt. The doctors tried many things hoping to help Lexi and lessen her pain, but not much worked. Many times a year, Lexi had to travel far away from her remote community for tests and treatments. She needed a helper to be by her side many hours throughout the day. Her doctors thought a service dog would be a valuable addition to Lexi's care. To Tessa, this seemed like the perfect opportunity for "Kids' Cookies for a Cause" to get involved. They were going to raise funds to help Lexi get a service dog!

Because so many people in town had heard about Lexi and wanted to help, cookie donations overflowed the table. The Coast Guard station did a fundraiser to help Lexi's family also. The community worked together to raise the most funds of any year yet.

And guess what? Lexi got a service dog and named her Iggy! Iggy was so sweet. She enjoyed getting smothered by Lexi's hugs and kisses. She retrieved things that Lexi needed and sometimes helped her walk. Iggy knew just how to comfort her girl when she was sad and in pain. Iggy even got to go to the hospital with Lexi, and no one minded that Iggy hopped right up in her bed. Everyone loved Iggy, but especially Lexi and her family.

Tessa's heart overflowed seeing Lexi and Iggy together. Serving others gave her such a feeling of purpose. She witnessed kindness being paid forward all around her. It was amazing how her tiny idea had sprouted wings and grown to help so many people. She was so thankful she had acted on that idea because it was changing her life and making a huge impact on the lives around her.

Tessa didn't stop after helping Lexi get her service dog. No way! The next year she helped raise almost $10,000 for the local Community Connections in addition to collecting dozens of bags of cold weather gear, which she helped disburse to the elderly and children and adults with disabilities. Other exciting things started happening, too. As Tessa's fundraiser grew, so did she. Not just in age and height, but in wisdom, experience, strength, and how much love she had to share. And do you know what else? Tessa was only twelve years old when she received a "Volunteer of the Year" award from the First Lady of her State.

She even traveled to her State's capital of Juneau, Alaska for a special ceremony and presentation.

Another time, she sat right next to Alaska's U.S. Senator Lisa Murkowski at a special dinner. Talking with the Senator about how community service helps build and strengthen

communities encouraged Tessa that her work was making
a difference far beyond her little island town. Her first-hand
experience proved that big obstacles were much easier
to overcome when people worked together
and supported each other.

In the year right before this book came out, Tessa chose "Casting for Recovery" to receive her fundraising money. She chose it because she knew a lot of people who had dealt with breast cancer. The women Tessa knew who had attended a previous retreat were challenged, strengthened, and blessed by all they had learned and the new friendships they made. The outpouring of love and donations from so many of the champion survivors along with friends and family blew Tessa away. You probably won't be surprised to learn that the fundraiser grew even beyond that of prior years--in cookie donations and actual funds raised--and set another fundraising record for "Kids' Cookies for a Cause."

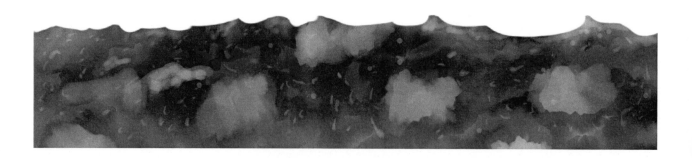

Now you know the story of Tessa and her little idea that she put into action. Just because this book has come to an end, however, doesn't mean the work is finished for Tessa or her "Kids' Cookies for a Cause." You'll have to check in on them to see how they are doing.

You are now left with some questions to ponder . . .
Can a cookie change the world?

Or, do you think it was the heart of the person behind the cookie that changed the world?

Whatever you end up deciding, know this for sure . . . if you have an idea that you think will help someone, do everything you can to act on it. Because if you do,
you can change the world, too.
Even if it's just one person, or one cookie, at a time.

Thank you for reading this book. Every book sold contributes to ALS Therapy Development Institute (ALS TDI) and to Tessa's fundraiser.
We tremendously appreciate your support.

Please turn the page for some discussion ideas and things to consider.

~Discussion Ideas~

1. Make a list of the things that you are really good at or really enjoy doing. These are called your talents and skills. Did you know you have a purpose here on earth and you were given those talents and skills to use to give back to the world and make it a better place?

2. Think about three people going through a difficult situation or season in their life. What can you do to help them? How can you use your talents and skills to act on your idea?

3. Is there a cause or something in your community or at your school that you could help with? If so, what is it and what can you do to make a difference? Be sure to share your ideas.

If you would like to share a story about someone who has made a difference in the world, please go to:

www.accentuatethepositivepublishing.com

There you can enter contact information and receive a form to submit your story with pictures. We will choose several stories each month to feature on our webpage, and...

You never know... maybe the next book could be about YOU!

~Glossary~

Hot commodity - Someone or something that is highly valued or in much demand.

Philanthropist - a person who seeks to promote the welfare of others, especially by the generous donation of money to good causes. Philanthropy is the love of humanity.

Information on some of the causes discussed in this book in the order they appear in the story.

ALS - Amyotrophic Lateral Sclerosis or Lou Gehrig's disease is a neurodegenerative disease that causes rapidly progressive muscle weakness. Specifically, the disease affects nerve cells (motor neurons) that control the muscles that enable you to move, speak, breathe and swallow.

ALS-tdi - (Therapy Development Institute) is dedicated to finding a cure for ALS.
https://www.als.net/

CRMO - Multifocal osteomyelitis, chronic; Chronic multifocal osteomyelitis - is a rare and serious disease. It involves inflammation of one or more bones and can be chronic. Symptoms can come and go. The immune system wrongly attacks normal bone and causes inflammation. If you go to the following website for CRMO Awareness, you will see a picture of little Lexi who was mentioned in our story. Lexi suffers with several different diagnoses in addition to CRMO. She is a sweet, brave little fighter and we sure hope and pray they find a way to put her disease into remission and eventually find a cure. http://crmoawareness.org

The Special Olympics athlete's oath, which was first introduced by Eunice Kennedy Shriver at the inaugural Special Olympics international games in Chicago in 1968, is "Let me win. But if I cannot win, let me be brave in the attempt." The motto of Special Olympics is about finding the courage to give it all you've got. https://www.specialolympics.org/

CfR or Casting for Recovery. Mission - The mission of Casting for Recovery® (CfR) is to enhance the

quality of life of women with breast cancer through a unique retreat program that combines breast cancer education and peer support with the therapeutic sport of fly fishing. The program offers opportunities for women to find inspiration, discover renewed energy for life and experience healing connections with other women and nature. CfR serves women of all ages, in all stages of breast cancer treatment and recovery, at no cost to participants.

Special art by local artist, Matt Hamilton, for Casting for Recovery Alaska - Ketchikan. Used with permission from the artist. You can see more of his work at:
www.creativehustlercompany.com

Tessa and Rhonda's Contact Info and Other Fun Tidbits

This story is about Tessa, an extraordinary 14-year-old philanthropist with a big heart for her neighbors and her local island community. When she was seven years old, Tessa told her mother she wanted to raise money for the local homeless shelter. From that moment, *Kids' Cookies for a Cause* was born. Due to Tessa's hard work, determination, and charitable spirit (and support from her family and friends), the program has grown significantly and is well-known throughout her Alaskan community. Tessa has given over $50,000 to local causes and charities with her fundraising.

Tessa is now in high school but still captains *Kids' Cookies for a Cause* each Christmas. She plays basketball, manages the wrestling team, and is active in school fundraisers, Pep Club, and Rotary Club. Tessa traveled to Fiji for a mission trip in the summer of 2017. With young leaders from all over the country, she served the communities there for three weeks where she helped build water-catchment systems, taught English to young children, and helped clean water waste. Tessa hopes to be an occupational therapist when she is older.

Tessa's favorite cookies are warm, chewy ginger snaps and she does not like dunking her cookies!

Tessa's email address is tessasalazar12@gmail.com. Check up on her continued fundraising and follow *Kids Cookies for a Cause* on Facebook at
https://www.facebook.com/groups/KidsCookiesForACause/

Author Rhonda Bolling has lived in Alaska for 23 years. She loves living in The Last Frontier with her very funny husband and her smart and kind twin daughters. She misses her grown son who recently moved from Alaska to Texas.
This is her second published book. She has also helped two other authors publish their books: *After Midnight Meditations*, by Barbara Kimball; and *The Day the Pudding Got Away*, by M.T. Cobblepott (aka Suzan Thompson).
A busy community volunteer and involved with her church and kids' ministry, Rhonda is also a member of *Now I Lay Me Down To Sleep*, which is a non-profit organization comprised of volunteer professional photographers certified to provide the healing gift of remembrance photography to parents suffering the loss of a baby.

Her favorite cookie is the chocolate pixie because it reminds her of her late grandmother. She does not dunk her cookies in milk or anything else, for that matter. One of Rhonda's biggest passions in life is to encourage people to live their best lives and give their best selves to the world around them. She believes that a little love, kindness, and thoughtfulness go a long way and that everyone has the potential to make the world a better place. Tessa's story exemplifies giving the best of oneself.

It brings Rhonda great joy to claim Tessa as her Goddaughter, and she is so proud of the incredible person Tessa is.

Visit the author's website to learn more and get links to a couple of Tessa's secret recipes.
www.rhondabolling.com or www.accentuatethepositivepublishing.com

Made in the USA
San Bernardino, CA
31 August 2018

CAN A COOKIE CHANGE THE WORLD?

70% OF NET PROCEEDS FROM SALES WILL BE DONATED TO CHARITIES*

A YOUNG GIRL SETS OUT TO HELP HER REMOTE ALASKAN TOWN AND ENDS UP IMPACTING THE WORLD IN WAYS SHE COULD NEVER HAVE IMAGINED.

JOIN TESSA ON A COURAGEOUS ADVENTURE AS SHE MAKES GREAT THINGS GROW FROM A SMALL IDEA.

LET YOURSELF AND YOUR CHILD BE INSPIRED BY THIS TRUE STORY THAT CONFRONTS THESE QUESTIONS: HOW CAN A CHILD MAKE A DIFFERENCE? CAN A COOKIE CHANGE THE WORLD?

35% OF THE NET PROCEEDS FROM THIS BOOK WILL BE GIVEN TO ALS THERAPY DEVELOPMENT INSTITUTE (ALS TDI) AND 35% WILL BE GIVEN TO TESSA'S FUNDRAISER.

AUTHOR ACADEMY elite

ISBN 9781640852327

9 781640 852327

T3-CBP-368